For Jennifer and Rebecca.

DIAL BOOKS FOR YOUNG READERS

An imprint of Penguin Random House LLC, New York

Text copyright © 2019 by Adam Rubin

Illustrations copyright © 2019 by Daniel Salmieri

Visit us online at penguinrandomhouse.com

ISBN 9780525428893 • Printed in China • 10 9 8 7 6 5 4 3 2 1

Designed by Jason Henry • Text set in Gotham

HIGH FIVE

ADAM RUBIN

illustrated by

DANIEL SALMIERI

DIAL BOOKS FOR YOUNG READERS

A high five is a handy way
for happy friends to say "hooray!"
A special slap to celebrate
when everything is going great.

But there's a contest held each year,
where high five fans from far and near
all press their palms against the rest,
to see whose high five is the best.

I was the greatest in my day,
and now I call myself Sensei.
I teach young fivers what to do...
my next apprentice could be you.

First, get your hands loose and limber
(you don't want to pull a finger).

Let's make sure you understand
how to position your hand:

Palm out
Fingers spread
Wrist straight
Elbow bent.

Next, we need to find a friend,
someone to high five against.
You cannot high five yourself—
that's called clapping, that won't help.

This is Glen the elephant.
He'll help your development.
Fingers very small in size,
but look close! He does have five.

Okay, kid, let's see what you've got—
give ol' Glen your very best shot.

He's got thick skin, he'll survive.
Ready or not...

I confess I'm impressed
with your zesty finesse,
but there is one last test
to assess nonetheless.

The success of our quest
rests on inventiveness.

Precious freshness is stressed,
as this chart will suggest.

THE CLASSIC

THE DOUBLE

THE WINDMILL

THE AIR FIVE

THE BETWEEN
THE LEGS

THE DOUBLE BEHIND
THE BACK SLAM

THE HIGH FOOT

THE NINJA TURTLE

THE SUPERMARKET
SWEEP

THE CELTIC KNOT

THE KING OF
THE JUNGLE

THE NYC

You'll have to show a little style
to make those high five judges smile:

A special look upon your face,
a striking pose or some cool phrase.
Express your creativity,
'cause that's the thing we want to see.

HIGH
FIVE!

Was that your new signature slap?
My grandma fives better than that!

Perhaps you didn't understand—
I don't want to see something bland.
I want to see something brand-new,
a high five only you would do.
A fresh technique
that's so unique,
it leaves me unable to speak...

HIGH FIVE!

That was a phenomenon!

My doubts about you are gone.
Now it's rest we focus on—
the tournament starts at dawn.

Can't sleep—too excited!
Dancing in my bed all through the night.
Can't sleep—too excited!
Dancing in my bed all through the night.

It's time to five, kid. Feast your eyes:
The best alive all here to try
to win that hand-shaped trophy prize
that once upon a time was mine.

Wiggle those fingers and look alive—
the championships have arrived!

ROUND 1
GIGANTIC THE BEAR
700 POUNDS OF HAIR

No complaining about her size.
remember your training—

Congratulations, you stood your ground!
Good solid contact and crisp rebound.

Your confidence helped you make it through—
one round down, now it's on to Round Two.

ROUND 2

KANGAROO PAUL

FASTEST HANDS OF THEM ALL

This marsupial loves to cheat
(he's known for his pouch of deceit).

Bouncing is just a distraction,
pay close attention to catch him.

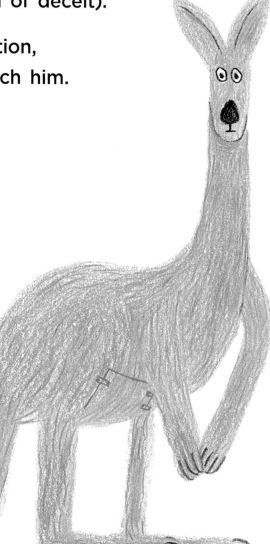

But this time, close your eyes.
Visualize, you guys:
See the hands in your mind.
Let those fingers fly blind.

Close your peepers
and keep 'em tight.
This will be outta sight. . . .

HIGH
FIVE!

That was the best five I've ever seen!
Well . . . it *sounded* like it was supreme.
I was so nervous for both of you,
I had to close my own eyes too.
But . . .
the judges say the winner is YOU!

It's a tie! My oh my.
Let's give it one more try...

The old one-two—
they can't trick you!
Double the points,
and move on through.

TIME FOR ROUND 3

WITH SHIFTY THE LIZARD

HE CAN DISAPPEAR, JUST LIKE A WIZARD

This guy will try to fool your eyes,
but only his skin is disguised.
He can't blend in that shifty grin,
and if you find him you will win.

How in the world did you see that?
Wow, I can hardly believe that.

You've made it halfway through your quest.
I wonder who will come up next?

ROUND 4

oh my gosh, it's Glen from the gym!

I guess I underestimated him.

You're both my friends, so no matter who wins,
respect one another. Bow to begin.
I wish you both could win that prize
but you can't, so let's do this—

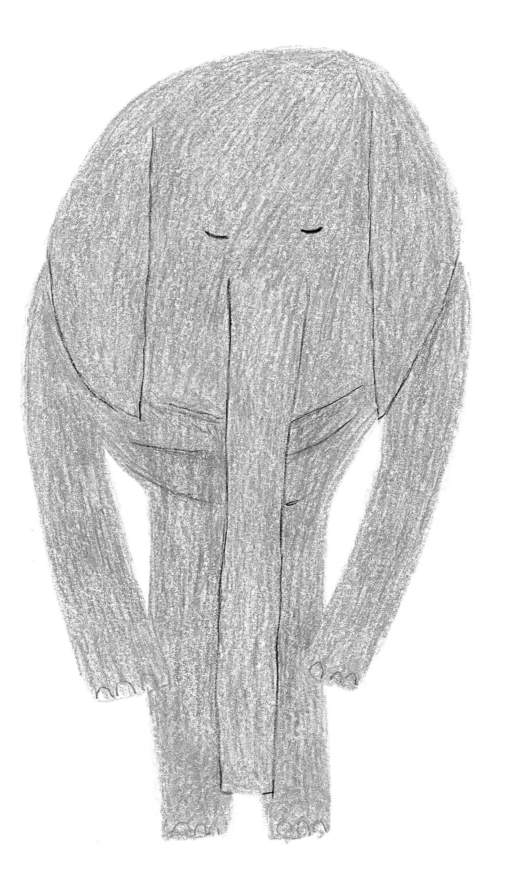

It's the final round.
Listen to the crowd:
"Make us proud, kid! Make us proud!"
Who could stop you now?

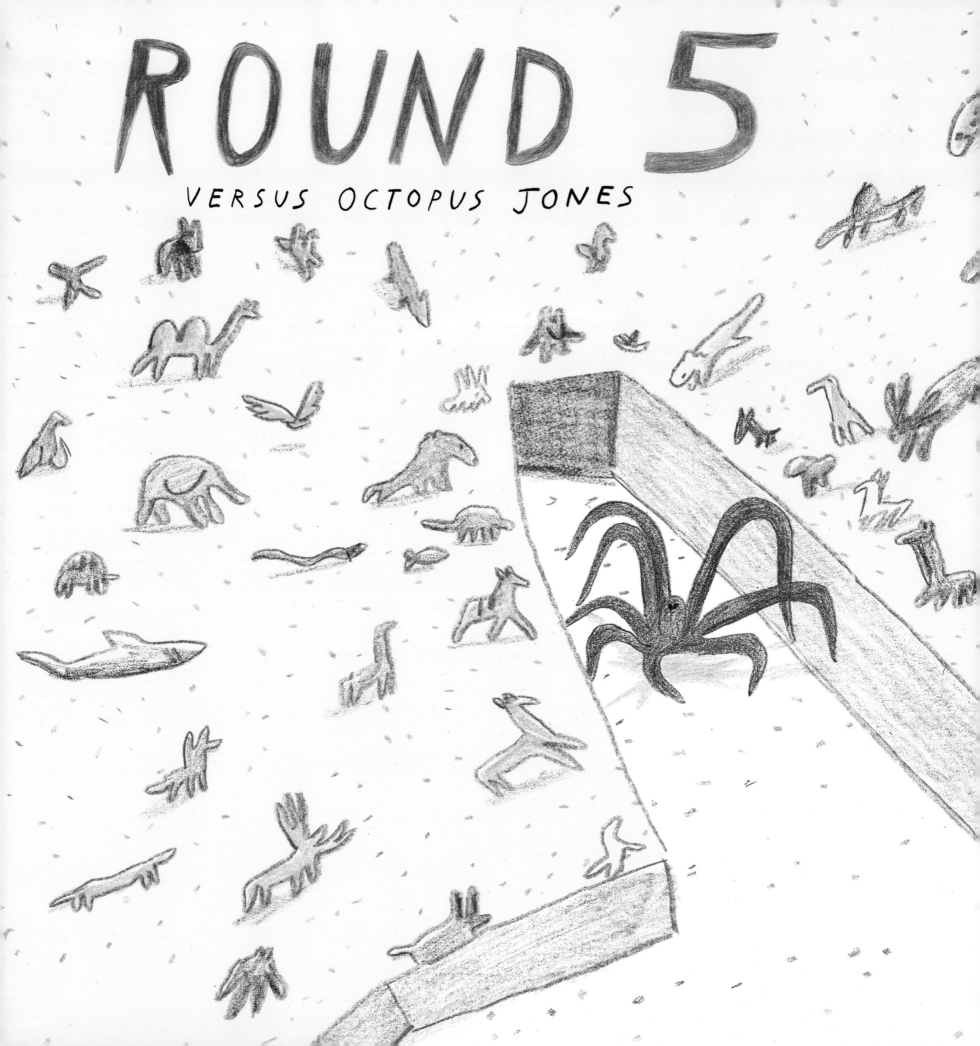

The crowd goes hush, somebody groans.

I've never seen this guy five—
they say he's the greatest alive.

He has eight hands, you just have two...
a little uneven, it's true.

But if anyone can beat him it's you!
Plus, his time to lose is way overdue.

I'll give you one tip to help win the game:
Focus your eyes on his elbows to aim...

What do you mean octopuses don't have elbows, Glen?
He's no marine biologist, don't listen to him.

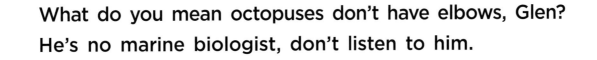

Just calm your nerves and concentrate
(and make sure you high five all eight).

That's how we spell...

You did it! You won!
The tournament's done!
Only one thing left to do:

Hold up your trophy
and shout out "woo-hoo!"
The new high five champ is you!